Fitting

Fitting

The CORNHUSK DOLL

The CORNHUSK DOLL

EVELYN MINSHULL

ILLUSTRATED BY EDWIN B. WALLACE

HERALD PRESS
Scottdale, Pennsylvania
Kitchener, Ontario

Library of Congress Cataloging-in-Publication Data

Minshull, Evelyn White.
  The cornhusk doll.

  Summary: Caught and injured in Pa's bear trap, an
Indian and his daughter are forced to stay with a
pioneer family, where hatred finally gives way to
friendship due to young Mary and her cornhusk doll.
  1. Indians of North America—Juvenile fiction.
[1. Indians of North America—Fiction. 2. Frontier
and pioneer life—Fiction. 3. Dolls—Fiction.
4. Friendship—Fiction] I. Wallace, Edwin B., ill.
II. Title.
PZ7.M673Co 1987   [E]   86-27125
ISBN 0-8361-3431-1

For Mikel Erin Barry
who communicates
love.

WHEN PA set the bear trap out back of the lean-to, no one figured he might catch an Indian in it.

Mary, hugging her cornhusk doll to the front of her flour-streaked apron, hated to think of anything being caught in those cruel iron jaws.

Jed, driving a stake through the chain's ring, hoped that the bear might have a cub young enough for taming.

Pa and Ma just wanted an end to the pig-killing which had been going on since early spring, when the old bear woke up and left her cave.

"She's sure a hungry one," Jed said.

Pa started scattering old leaves to cover the ugly trap jaws. "All critters have a right to eat, son," he said. "And that includes us. If we don't stop that bear, there'll be no pork to go with our beans next winter."

He stooped down, the way he often did when he talked to Mary, and hugged her over against his knee.

"Mighty fine-looking young'un you have there, Ma'am," he said, touching his finger to the doll's embroidered nose.

Mary smiled, forgetting her sad thoughts about the bear and the trap.

Her father had made the cornhusk doll himself during the long evenings of the past winter. Ma had embroidered the eyes, nose, and mouth, and adjusted the corn silk hair.

And Jed had made the doll a tiny pair of deerhide moccasins, just like the ones he and Pa wore for hunting.

"What's her name this week?" Pa asked.

"Still Annabelle," answered Mary. "Annabelle Mehitabel Carstairs."

"Hmmmm-hmmmmm!" Pa approved, pushing himself to his feet. "A mighty fine name, too."

He swung off toward the cabin, his long legs covering the ground faster than Jed could keep up at a trot.

Just for a moment, Mary looked at the leaf-covered spot where the hidden trap lay. She imagined the hungry bear, moving fast along her path toward a young-pig dinner . . . stepping on the leaves . . . SNAP!

She closed her eyes and held Annabelle tight. Then, trying not to think of the bear's pain, she ran off toward the stream where she and Annabelle liked to play and watch minnows.

Pa was right, she knew. They did have to save their little pigs. They did have to get rid of that bear.

The old bear was a smart one, though. Somehow, she seemed to know that the trap was there. She just began a new path on the other side of the lean-to and kept on killing Pa's pigs.

One night, Pa heard the racket and got off a shot. The bear ran away, but left a little pig behind, dead.

Mary and Annabelle watched, next day, while Jed and Pa moved the trap.

Pa straightened up, rubbing his back, when the trap was all covered again.
"That should catch us a bear," Jed said.

But it caught them an Indian instead.

The Indian was from the village just across the mountains, Pa figured, because he and his little girl were traveling on foot.

Pa and Jed had packed over the mountains once to visit the village. The Indians there spoke some English, Pa remembered.

"Who are you?" Pa asked carefully, after he and Jed had sprung the trap, after they'd helped the Indian to their cabin, and after Ma had tended the ugly wounds where the trap had bitten into flesh and crushed bone.

"What is your name?"

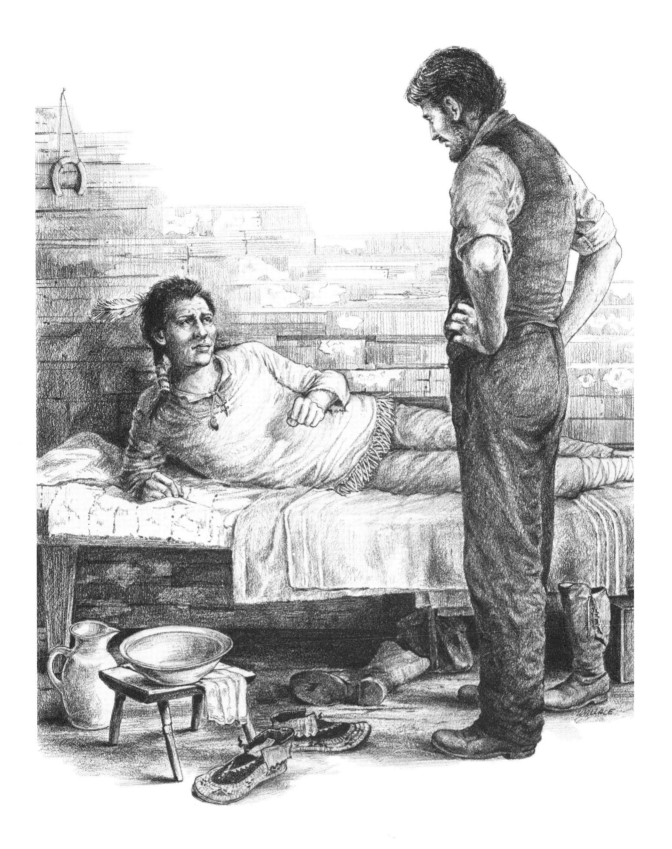

The Indian just lay on Jed's cot and glared at Pa as though he hated him worse than hunger.

"Do you not understand me?" asked Pa slowly, but the Indian never blinked an eye.

"I don't think he does, Pa," Jed said. "He must come from some other village, after all."

"Poor man," Ma said sadly. "What a terrible thing to have happened to him! And what will his little girl do?"

"We'll give them both good care while he heals," Pa said. "The wound's clean. It's a shame it happened, but it's done. It could have been worse."

Sitting on the step stool, Mary looked quickly at the small Indian girl, standing at the edge of the cot beside her father.

She was pretty with her small-boned figure, her glossy black hair, and her large eyes, as dark as wet bearskin.

Her dress was dirty, with some of her father's blood dried on the front and on her hands from when she'd tried to spring the trap.

"I wish she could understand us," Ma said softly, "so we could tell
her how sorry we are."

"There are other ways than talk," Pa said. "Maybe there are even
better ways to show that you want to be friends."

Mary slid off the step stool. "I'll take her to our stream, and she can wash the blood off there, and watch the minnows swimming around."

Pa smiled his approval, and Ma pushed Mary gently toward the cot. The little Indian girl watched her coming, her eyes brightening as Mary held out the cornhusk doll.

Mary kept her glance on the little girl's face. She didn't once look at the older Indian, and Jed's warning came too late.

Just as Jed yelled, "Watch out, Mary!" the Indian's unhurt foot flashed out and caught her hard in the ribs, flinging her sideways against the slab table.

She fell with a little cry to the hard-packed dirt floor. Her ribs felt as though they'd been squashed with Ma's rolling pin.

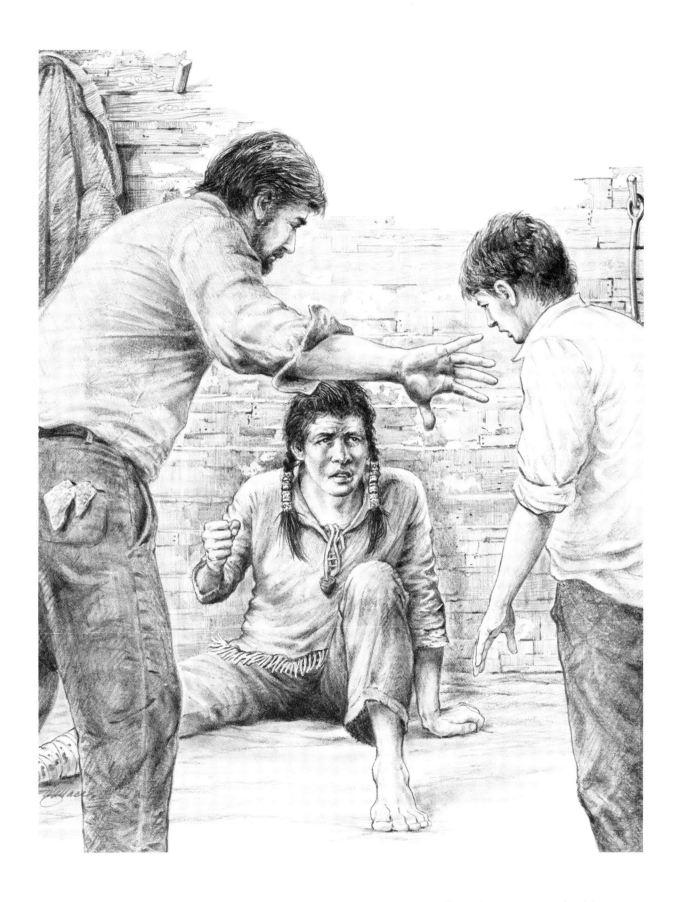

"How dare you!" Jed yelled, and ran at the Indian, but Pa caught him and held him back.

"He didn't understand, son," Pa said quietly, while he watched Ma comfort Mary. "We were the cause of his being hurt, and he didn't understand that Mary only meant to be friends with his little girl."

"Are you all right, Mary girl?" Pa asked.

Mary tried not to show how much it hurt when she stooped to pick up Annabelle. She looked over every inch of her doll before she answered, "We're both all right, Pa."

Ma said, "Land sakes, he burst his wounds open worse, thrashing about like that!"

"If we could only make him understand," sighed Pa. "If we could only show him that we want to be his friends."

"Yellow Feather does not want white man for friend!"

It took all of them a minute to realize that it was the Indian who had spoken . . . that he was speaking English!

"Why, he does too understand!" Jed shouted. "He knew every word we said before, and he kicked Mary out of pure meanness!"

"My people know more about white folks than their language," Yellow Feather said in a cold voice. "We know that whites stole our land, our animals.

"The trap which hurt my leg was set for bear. Once, all bears belonged to my people. White folks have taken everything and given nothing but hate.

"My daughter and I reply with hate for all white people!"

Pa stepped forward and said softly, "White people aren't all alike,
any more than every tree is alike . . . or every sunset."

"Wolves are all alike," the Indian said. "To trust a wolf would be foolish, and Yellow Feather is no fool."

Ma cleared her throat nervously and said, "Mary, come help me set a meal."

Yellow Feather raised his voice to follow her to the black stove where her mother was frying sausage.

"We will eat your food because we must," Yellow Feather shouted.

"But each moment we stay here—and long after we have gone—we will pray that your cabin burns to the ground . . . and that all of you die of sickness and hunger."

Mary drew a deep, shocked breath. She had never heard such cruel words before. She had never heard such a cruel voice before. She had

never seen anyone look – even at a rattlesnake – the way Yellow Feather was looking at each of them.

Glancing at the little Indian girl, Mary saw the dark eyes filling with tears and spilling over.

Mary knew that the little girl did not feel that way. Mary smiled at her. The little girl stared through her tears, and then smiled slowly back.

"Mary," her mother was saying, "mix up the corn bread, please."

THE INDIAN'S wounds healed slowly. Day after day, hate burned in his eyes. Night after night – except those nights when Jed and Pa kept guard outside, near the pigs – the old bear came around. But she never walked near the trap.

Some nights, Pa heard the bear in time to scare her off.

But often the bear killed and carried away another young pig without anyone hearing.

Anyone except Yellow Feather, Mary thought. She could almost tell by looking at him each morning if they would find another young pig gone. He would be smiling coldly.

He's glad Pa's lost another pig, Mary thought, and hate began to rise within her, too.

"Hating is always wrong," Ma told Mary and Jed one night just before bedtime. "God wants us to repay evil with good. It isn't easy, but it's what he wants."

Mary was sure that it would be impossible to feel love for anyone like Yellow Feather. She did think, though, that she could learn to love the little Indian girl.

Sometimes, when her father was sleeping on the cot, the Indian girl walked outside, stretching her arms to the sky, picking wild flowers, or stooping to pick up pretty pebbles.

Mary and Annabelle often walked with her. Sometimes the two girls talked, but quietly, so that Yellow Feather wouldn't waken.

Yellow Feather caught them only once. His leg had healed enough that he could leave the cot for a few minutes and hobble about.

One day, when the girls were coming back from the stream, they saw him leaning in the cabin doorway, watching. Both girls stopped in dismay.

"Let's run away," Mary suggested in a frightened whisper. "He's looking at you the way he looks at us . . . as though he hates you, too. He couldn't ever catch us. . . ."

But, when he called her, Yellow Feather's daughter walked slowly to him and bowed her head.

Each evening after that, while Ma taught love from the Bible to her children, Yellow Feather talked to his daughter.

"White people know love only for themselves and their own kind," he said. "To trust them is to be a fool."

Slowly, the little girl smiled less often at Mary. Even when her father was asleep, if she saw Mary coming, she would walk away.

"Soon, she'll be as filled with hate as he is," Ma sighed. "I wish we could help her. . . ."

"If we had more time—" began Mary, hugging Annabelle close.

"But we don't," said Pa. "In another few days, Yellow Feather will be well enough to walk away from here."

"Good riddance," Jed muttered, kicking at a nut which had fallen to the floor.

"Son—" began Pa, and then didn't say anything more, but just sighed.

Those last two days, Mary tried harder than ever to be a friend to the little Indian girl. She became sadder and sadder when she found that her friendship wasn't wanted anymore.

It seemed to Mary that Annabelle was sad, too. Not only because Yellow Feather and his daughter would not be friendly, but because this might be the last time any white person would have a chance to offer them friendship.

How sad that they could not all be friends.

That last morning, Pa added to his family's quiet sadness. He told them that the bear had killed another little pig the night before.

A cold smile twisted Yellow Feather's lips. His daughter's smile seemed much like his.

"That bear will kill all of your animals," he said. "It is our wish."

Pa said quietly, "It is our hope that happiness will go with you wherever you walk."

Yellow Feather looked surprised for a moment, then he laughed.
"White folks always find words of friendship easy. Their words are
like deerskin rug spread over quicksand."

The little girl's chin went up and her dark eyes flashed. "We are not fools," she said.

Suddenly, Mary wanted desperately to prove her love to the Indian girl. But how could she, unless she had something to give besides words?

Mary had nothing which was all her own. Nothing – except
Annabelle. She smiled down at her cornhusk doll and hugged her close.
Then her smile and her fingers stiffened.

She wanted to give something, and Annabelle was all she had to give.

Mary knew that if she stopped to think about it, she could never give Annabelle away.

She thrust the doll quickly toward the startled Indian girl. "I want you to have her," Mary said through her tears. "Please love her— Please...."

Mary turned away, letting the tears fall.

The cabin was still except for her quiet crying, the crackle of the breakfast logs in the fireplace, and the scrape, scrape of Jed's toe across the floor.

Then Mary felt a hand on her shoulder.

Dear Pa, she thought, and turned.

But it was not Pa who stood there, looking down at her with eyes which asked questions and a mouth which was smiling in a warm way.

"I was wrong," Yellow Feather said softly. "Some white people can give love. Like the Indian, white folks not all the same . . . even as sunsets are different."

Gently, he pressed Annabelle into Mary's hands.

"If your father will teach how doll is made," he said, "I will show how to trap a pig-killing bear."

Yellow Feather offered his hand to Pa, and Pa shook it.

Smiling, the little Indian girl came to Mary and they linked arms and
spun around and around.

Yellow Feather was saying, "Only a fool turns from true friendship
when it appears . . . and Yellow Feather is no fool."

The Author

The Illustrator

Evelyn and Fred Minshull from Mercer, Pennsylvania, are the grandparents of young Mikel Erin Barry to whom this book is dedicated. They have three grown daughters: Valerie Courtney, Melanie Barry, and Robin Navaroli.

Originally an art education teacher with a degree from Edinboro College, Evelyn found—in the nonteaching years when her children were young—that a deeper love lay in writing. With her husband's encouragement, she survived the trauma of rejection slips to see hundreds of short stories, articles, plays, and poems reach print. *The Cornhusk Doll* is her twelfth book.

A return to teaching in 1967 allowed her to exercise both interests—English with high school students and art in the lower elementary grades. (She received a master's degree in English from Slippery Rock College in 1972.) In the late 1970s a new teaching assignment was added—coordination of a gifted program for grades K through 12. After twenty years at Commodore Perry School, Hadley, Pennsylvania, Evelyn continues in those three areas, as well as with five active extracurricular groups.

Her teaching of writing extends far beyond the local classroom—in writing workshops for groups from elementary through college, from prisoners through in-service programs for teachers. A long-term association with St. Davids Christian Writers' Conference has resulted in several terms on their board and many years of conference teaching.

Evelyn is a certified lay speaker and an active member of Vincent United Methodist Church, Jackson Center, Pa.

Edwin B. Wallace, artist and ordained minister in the Wesleyan Church, is a native of Pennsylvania. Drawing has been an important part of his life for as long as he can remember. He recalls as a young teenager sketching people in the pews (an activity he does not recommend) and then testing the accuracy of his efforts by asking persons after church to identify his drawings.

As a young illustrator, Wallace was particularly fascinated by the wildlife art of such greats as Charles Livingston Bull, Lynn Bogue Hunt, and Paul Bransom. He had his first public showing of animal drawings at age fifteen in Sharon, Pennsylvania. A feature article in *The Sharon Herald* (Jan. 1937) noted that "art critics, impressed with his technique and workmanship, predict for him a career as an illustrator."

While a freshman in high school, he began attending evening art classes taught by outstanding Pittsburgh artist/teacher Frank Smolen.

During thirty-plus years of pastoral and evangelistic ministry, Wallace used his talent to illustrate sermons and songs with chalk drawings and paintings. His work has appeared widely in religious periodicals, curriculum, and books.

One of his most challenging assignments was the commission by the Board of General Superintendents of the Wesleyan Church to do a composite portrait of the three principal founders of the presently merged church for the 200th anniversary celebration of the founding of Methodism in North America. The painting now hangs in the World Methodist Gallery/Museum at Lake Junaluska, North Carolina.